ADVENTURES OF

Ferguson

THE LITTLE RED FOX

Written and Illustrated by

GLENDA LORD-WRIGHT

Trilogy Christian Publishers
A Wholly Owned Subsidiary of Trinity Broadcasting Network
2442 Michelle Drive
Tustin, CA 92780

Cover design by: Glenda Lord-Wright

For information, address Trilogy Christian Publishing
Rights Department, 2442 Michelle Drive, Tustin, Ca 92780.
Trilogy Christian Publishing/ TBN and colophon are trademarks of Trinity Broadcasting Network.

For information about special discounts for bulk purchases, please contact Trilogy Christian Publishing.

Manufactured in the United States of America

Trilogy Disclaimer: The views and content expressed in this book are those of the author and may not necessarily reflect the views and doctrine of Trilogy Christian Publishing or the Trinity Broadcasting Network.

10 9 8 7 6 5 4 3 2 1

Library of Congress Cataloging-in-Publication Data is available.

ISBN 978-1-63769-562-3 (Print Book)
ISBN 978-1-63769-563-0 (ebook)

Coming Soon

Adventures of Ferguson: the Little Red Fox
Lake Butte Overlook

Adventures of Ferguson: the Little Red Fox
Firehole Canyon

Come follow me on the adventures of Ferguson, a curious little red fox and his unlikely friends.

Ferguson has the best of friends: a mischievous magpie named Maggie, a badger named Duff, and three crazy squirrels named Elvis-Anne, Lily, and Nigel.

Unlikely, unusual, and perfect together as they explore the magnificent Yellowstone National Park. There's an unusual family adoption, helping a sick friend, and several more unexpected events.

So come on, follow me on the adventures of Ferguson and his friends!

Soli Deo gloria

Hi, I'm Ferguson!

CHAPTER 1

Crisp, cool winds swirl through the aspen trees. Ferguson, the little red fox, awakens to find the sun shining into the family den. As he looks out, sunlight on the leaves creates an abundance of blazing autumn colors of reds, oranges, and yellows. The leaves glow like they are alive!

Ferguson loves autumn, and his home in Yellowstone National Park is the best place to live. The air is cooler, colors are spectacular, and everyone is more playful!

Ferguson's best friend is a black-and-white magpie named Maggie. Her shiny black feathers shimmer dark blue when the sun shines on them, making her white feathers appear even whiter.

Ferguson and Maggie have been friends since Maggie was a baby bird. Their friendship began shortly after Mama and Papa built their den at the base of a large fir tree. Early that spring, Maggie fell out of her nest that sits high up in the aspen trees close to the fox den. Being too young to fly, the only thing she can do is find a small crevice to hide in at the base of the tree.

Hearing a new sound, Ferguson and his younger twin brothers scurry out of their den to investigate. The young foxes lift their noses to catch smells riding on the breeze. As they look around, they see a tiny black-and-white feathery ball with big dark eyes at the base of the tree looking back at them.

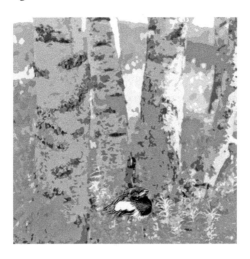

Now the foxes' curiosity got the best of them. Time to investigate!

Maggie finds herself surrounded by three young red fox. Cautiously she watches, not knowing what else to do. She scoots back as far as she can against the tree and curls up as small as she can.

Their bellies low to the ground, Ferguson's twin brothers creep slowly toward her. Stretching out their little black noses, they sniff and sniff as their tails whip back and forth. Maggie watches their twitching little noses, thinking how funny they look. She laughs out loud—which comes out more like a little squeal than a laugh.

The twins jump when Maggie laughs, which makes Maggie laugh again. Deciding there is nothing dangerous about this little feathery ball, they inch their way closer. All of a sudden, sounds in the nearby bushes distract the twins. They jump, knocking each other over, and then scamper toward the bushes. They quickly forget about the feathery ball at the base of the tree.

Maggie realizes these red furry four-legged animals are only curious. She relaxes and shakes out her feathers. Laughing out loud, she wonders what makes them act so silly.

The twins stop and turn around when they hear her squealing laugh again. They venture back over to the little black-and-white feathery ball. Maggie watches them closely, curling up tight against the tree again, not sure what they will do next.

Ferguson, who is standing back and watching, slowly steps closer and begins talking to her so she won't be scared.

"Hi, my name is Ferguson, and these are my twin brothers. You don't need to be afraid. We're not going to hurt you. We heard noises and came out to see what it was. Did you fall out of the tree? Are you okay?"

Maggie nods her little head. "My name is Maggie," she says quietly. "I am a magpie, and I'm all alone. Mama and Papa are gone, and I don't know what happened to them. They haven't returned for a long time."

Maggie, being so young and not knowing how to fly, cannot return to the safety of her nest. She is too young to take care of herself.

Ferguson walks over to sit next to Maggie. "I am sorry about your Mama and Papa. Family is important," he says, "and I don't know what I would do without mine." After a few moments, Ferguson gets up and walks over to his brothers. They huddle together and begin to whisper among themselves.

Turning back to Maggie, Ferguson says, "We have a great idea, Maggie. Come live with us. You can be our sister. Mama and Papa will take good care of you, and we'll help too!"

Young Maggie looks at them with wide eyes, so surprised at what he said. "I didn't think birds and fox could be friends. Are you sure you won't eat me?" asks Maggie.

Ferguson and his brothers look at each other and burst out laughing. "Eat you? Of course not—we won't eat you! Anyway, there's nothing to eat. You're just a baby fuzz ball with legs and a beak. Besides, we like you."

The rest of the day, they laugh and play together. Maggie watches her new friends. She notices there is something special about Ferguson. Being the oldest, he watches while his twin brothers continue their rambunctious wrestling. He stays close, watching over Maggie too, and this is the day their friendship began.

The sun is lowering in the sky and will soon disappear behind the mountains. The edges of the clouds are glowing golden yellow, the air is cooling quickly, and the light of day is dimming. Ferguson calls his brothers and puts little Maggie on his shoulder. It's time to head home and introduce her to Mama and Papa.

CHAPTER 2

Ferguson's twin brothers scamper ahead and run into their den, yelling, "Mama! Papa! Come quick. We have a new friend. Her name is Maggie, and she's all alone. She don't have a Mama or a Papa. Can she stay with us? *Pleeeease?* We don't have a sister, and she has nowhere to stay and no one to take care of her. She's just a baby bird, and she can't even fly yet. She's a magpie, and she's pretty! Can she stay? Can she?"

"Slow down, boys!" Mama says, laughing at their excitement.

While they continue telling Mama and Papa about Maggie, Ferguson gently guides her down into the den. Maggie is nervous and shaking all over. She has never been underground or in a fox den before. Ferguson whispers reassuringly to her that she is safe and everything is okay.

Mama and Papa greet Maggie warmly. "Come in, Maggie. Welcome to our home. We are getting ready for dinner," Mama says. Further discussions about Maggie living with them will have to wait. It's time to eat, and they are hungry!

They gather around the table and hold paws as Papa says a prayer of thanks to God for his family, their home and food, and their newest little guest, Maggie. She silently sits on the table next to Ferguson, watching in amazement.

The foxes eagerly chatter all through dinner. They tell Mama and Papa where they found Maggie and how they played all day. As they share their evening meal, Maggie nibbles slowly on her food as she quietly looks around. She has stopped shaking but is still nervous.

Mama and Papa include her in their conversations with the boys. This is quite different from what she is used to. She misses her family very much, but now that she has nowhere to go, she hopes that Mama and Papa will let her stay.

Maggie watches as Mama and Papa keep looking at each other and whispering all through dinner. Not understanding what they are quietly saying to each other leaves Maggie with an uneasy feeling again. The longer she sits here, the more she realizes how hungry she really is. Hastily she eats her food until everything on her plate is gone.

After dinner is over, the boys know what comes next—Mama cooks and they clean. Everyone has a part in this family. They help wash the dishes, wipe the table, and sweep the floor while Papa brings in logs to build a fire in their fireplace.

Maggie hops over to Mama and nervously looking down at the ground and softly says, "Thank you for having me in your home and sharing dinner with me."

Mama smiles down at her and says, "You are welcome, Maggie."

Maggie looks up and says, "I really like Ferguson and the twins. They are funny and fun to play with. Ferguson is thoughtful and kind too. He watched over the twins all afternoon. He stayed close and watched over me too."

Mama holds out her arms and welcomes Maggie with a warm hug. She holds her gently and wraps her long fluffy tail around Maggie. She whispers in her ear that she is sorry she has lost her Mama and Papa and hopes Maggie feels safe in their home.

Maggie looks up with big tears in her eyes and quietly says, "I do feel safe. Thank you."

Ferguson and his twin brothers watch as Mama hugs Maggie. Looking at each other, they wonder what they are saying.

With the kitchen cleanup finished, they gather around the fireplace with happy, full bellies while Papa settles into his comfortable evening chair. This is Papa's favorite place to sit. Sitting next to the big fireplace with his family around him makes Papa happy—Mama too.

Soon, the fire begins to dance and sizzle. Logs pop in the fireplace. Sparks drift up the chimney out into the air to become new stars in the night sky. They sit quietly, anxiously waiting for Papa to begin his evening story.

Papa tells the best stories! Sometimes they are funny, sometimes they are about their home in Yellowstone National Park, and sometimes they are about how important it is to help others in the woods. It doesn't matter what the story is about, as long as Papa is the one telling it.

This is a new experience for Maggie. Maggie is used to a quiet evening in her family's tiny nest snuggled tightly together. Ferguson looks at Maggie and sees she is calmer and no longer afraid.

After Papa finishes his story, Mama walks over to sit next to him, silently looking at each other. Ferguson and his brothers watch and wait. Maggie sits quietly, not knowing what to think. She starts to feel nervous again as she looks back and forth between Ferguson and Mama and Papa. Ferguson scoots Maggie closer to him, wrapping his fuzzy tail around her like a big warm hug. The quietness of the night, the crackling fire, and Ferguson next to her is comforting to Maggie.

Mama and Papa turn and look at her. Papa says, "Little Maggie, we are so glad that you are here. You and the boys had such a fun day together, and we're sure you'll have many more. Mama and I have been talking and wonder how would you feel about living with us?"

Maggie can hardly believe what she is hearing! She looks at Ferguson and the twins with eyes so big and wide and then turns back to Mama and Papa. She is so excited, she begins hopping up and down, and then looking at them with eyes so wide, she screeches out, "REALLY?"

Papa and Mama laugh and nod. "Yes. Really! We want to adopt you into our family." Mama continues, "We will feed and take care of you and raise you as our own. Is this something you would like?"

She hops over to Mama and Papa and wraps her little wings around them as far as she can and hugs them as tightly as a little bird can hug. With tears in her eyes, she looks up at them and screeches, "OH, I WOULD LIKE THAT A LOT—I REALLY WOULD! THANK YOU! THANK YOU SO MUCH!"

Everyone burst out laughing.

After a few moments, Maggie shyly looking up at them and says, "I have a question."

Papa replies, "What is it, little one?"

"Would it be okay if I call you Mama and Papa now?" Maggie asks softly.

They both reply, "Of course, you can!" hugging her gently while sounds of excitement fill their den. Ferguson and his little brothers gather around Maggie, giving her hugs too. Maggie will never forget this moment. She has a family again—Mama and Papa and three brothers!

From that day on, Ferguson and Maggie are inseparable. They become the best of friends and spend every waking moment together. Of course, the twins tag along, causing havoc and mischief at every opportune moment.

CHAPTER 3

As the days pass, the boys and Maggie are growing in size and in their personalities. Ferguson is becoming more curious. He finds great hiding places, sneaks up on Maggie without her realizing it, and leads his twin brothers on crazy races through the woods, over rocky hills, across streams, and back around again. Ferguson is growing into a responsible big brother, protecting and helping his little brothers and sister.

Over the next several weeks, Ferguson, Maggie, and the twins explore open fields, the woods, and streams nearby. Within a short time, Maggie learns to fly, thanks to other birds in the woods.

Maggie loves flying! Each day, she is becoming stronger and more agile, but there are many things that distract her. She finds coins and jewelry and pieces of colorful shiny glass—especially by the streams. The sun makes them sparkle and shine, and as soon as Maggie spots those sparkles, she's off on a new adventure of her own, for nothing distracts her more than something shiny!

Maggie is quite curious about *everything*! She is inquisitive and playful and ventures into situations she should think about first—like the time she ventured too close to two porcupines arguing or when several magpies were fighting over dinner. That didn't turn out too well for Maggie. Ferguson teased her about it, but she knew it is all in fun.

The unlikely duo of Ferguson and Maggie continuously catches the attention of others in the woods because foxes and birds do not coexist. Ferguson and Maggie are different in many ways and that makes them the best kind of friends.

It seems like everyone in the woods knows who they are. This is good—and bad! Good because their unique friendship helps others see they can get along—even with their differences—and become good friends too. The tales the woodland animals tell about Ferguson and Maggie are heard all around Yellowstone National Park.

Like I say, this is good and bad because they are always noticed. The mischief they get into is also talked about throughout the woodland and word always gets back to Mama and Papa. Truth be told, Maggie is the one who is getting into mischief and Ferguson is the one who is getting her out of trouble!

CHAPTER 4

This morning as Ferguson awakes, he thinks to himself, *There is something special in the air today. I can feel it!* He laughs as he listens to all the noises coming from the kitchen. He hears his twin brothers scampering around and laughing reasonably; sure they're playing and not being helpful at all.

Ferguson is quite hungry, and the smells coming from the kitchen are making his stomach growl. Just then, Mama calls out, "Time for breakfast!"

They all come running and jumping to their places around the table. They begin filling their bowls with Mama's steaming bread pudding and roasted acorns. Mama's bread pudding is Ferguson's favorite breakfast. In the middle of the table is a big bowl of Juneberries. He can't wait to pile them on top of his bread pudding. Fresh, cold water from the stream fills their cups.

Ferguson smiles at Mama and says, "Thank you, Mama. This is going to be *delicious*!"

Papa and Mama join paws, and the kids join too. It is time for Papa to say a prayer of thanks to God for his family, their home, and their food. They eat and talk and laugh. A short time later, breakfast is finished, the kitchen cleaned, and Ferguson is almost ready for the adventures of his day.

He pokes his head out of the den. Looking up into the vivid blue sky, he sees Maggie sitting high up in an aspen tree, sunning herself and waiting for him to come out to play. Somehow, she escaped outdoors, and he didn't notice. *How did she do that?* he wonders. She is becoming the great escape artist!

He wonders what kind of fun they will have today and what mischief Maggie will get into. He shakes his head and laughs to himself. Maggie makes him laugh a lot!

Before Ferguson can go back into the den, he hears, "Ferguson, ooohhh, Ferguson!" Maggie calls out, "Hurry up, we've got lots of exploring to do."

Ferguson replies, "I'll be back in a minute. I've got to finish cleaning up the bedroom."

"Why does it take you so long?" whines Maggie. "Be responsible later. We've got so much to explore. You're wasting daylight, Big Brother. COME ON!"

He quickly finishes making his bed and picks up the twigs and straw. As he looks around, he knows Mama and Papa will be pleased.

Turning to head out and catch up with Maggie, Ferguson hears her cawing, "FERRRGUSON, COME ON!"

Running out of their den, he shakes his head and laughs. "I'm here, Miss Impatient!"

"Ferguson, don't call me that. You know I don't like sitting around when there are so many things to see and do," says Maggie.

Ferguson replies, "You don't just want to go exploring, you want to see what kind of mischief you can get into today."

Huffing loudly, Maggie fluffs her tail feathers and stares at him. "That is unfair of you to say that, Ferguson. You know I don't go looking for trouble. It just finds me, and I can't help myself."

Ferguson looks at Maggie and cracks up laughing! "Oh, Maggie, if only that was true. You know how *not* to get into trouble," says Ferguson. "You just react without thinking and 'that' gets you in trouble," he chuckles. "I don't want anything to happen to you or for you to get into a dangerous situation or for either of us to get in trouble."

"Oh, Ferguson, I'm not going to get in trouble—at least not bad trouble. What could be so dangerous? Everyone in the woodland knows us, and they would help to protect us," says Maggie.

"Maggie, if you are to get into a dangerous situation, you are not the only one that can get hurt. If someone helping you gets hurt, how will you feel? I have to stop and think about things even when I'm excited about doing what I want to do. I need to think about our little brothers and you and Mama and Papa," says Ferguson.

"Wow, that's a lot to think about," Maggie says.

"It is and it isn't," replies Ferguson.

"What do you mean?" Maggie tilts her head and looks up at him with questioning eyes.

"Maggie, Mama and Papa teach us new things every day. Things to do and not to do. Then when we talk about them, we'll know what to do."

Maggie, with a big sigh, plops down with her little feet in front of her and stares at the ground. "Ferguson, you're right. I get so excited and want to see everything. I promise I will make better decisions about what I am going to do and to others and being helpful and—"

"Maggie?" interrupts Ferguson.

Looking up at him with her big black eyes, Maggie replies, "Yes, Ferguson?"

"You are my Little Sister, and I love you. We look out for each other, and we can do this together. Okay?"

"You are the *best* Big Brother in the woodland, Ferguson, and I love you too," Maggie says with a quiver in her voice.

"Come on, Little Sister, it's time to have some fun!" Ferguson says with a smile as he takes off running.

No matter how fast Ferguson runs, Maggie always flies faster—and she likes that!

CHAPTER 5

The day is young, and the sun is warm and bright with autumn's crisp, earthy fragrance drifting through the air. Maggie flies above the treetops watching Ferguson running below. She glides easily through the air and soars around and around while Ferguson runs around the trees and jumps over rocks and through the leaves, making them fly up in the air just to watch them float down again.

What a fun day this is going to be, Maggie thinks as she smiles to herself.

Ferguson is having a wonderful time as he keeps an eye on Maggie flying above. He is proud of her and thinks back to the day they found her. She is a perfect fit in their family.

Yellowstone Lake is just ahead, and Ferguson calls out to Maggie, "Let's go over to the lake. I'm thirsty."

Maggie takes a shallow dive and glides effortlessly to the rocky shore landing as Ferguson trots up beside her. They walk to the water's edge and step in. It feels wonderful! They take a big long drink as the cool waters lap against their feet and watch as a few of autumn's colorful leaves float by.

Even with autumn setting in, there are still a lot of visitors in the park. Ferguson and Maggie keep their distance as they listen to the squeals of excited children that echo across the lake. They rest together next to a huge spruce tree while Maggie leans against Ferguson. He wraps his fluffy tail around her like a big protective hug and listens to the gentle lapping of the water as it rolls the pebbles back and forth on the shore.

"Ferguson?" says Maggie.

"Yes, Maggie," Ferguson replies.

"Do you ever wonder what those visitors are like? I wonder if we can understand what they are saying. If we get closer to them, but not too close, do you think they will be friendly to us?" asks Maggie.

"Maaaggie, we've had this discussion before, so don't get any of your crazy ideas!" replies Ferguson. "You know we can't get close to the visitors. It is not safe for us."

"But, Ferguson, I just want to get close enough to hear what they're saying," Maggie whines.

"Absolutely not!" says Ferguson. "We can go anywhere we want, but we cannot be with people." Maggie sighs deeply. Ferguson pulls her closer and wraps his tail around her a little tighter.

They rest a while longer before they head back into the woods. A short distance away, Maggie calls out, "Ferguson, look, Juneberries!"

Juneberries

"I'm so hungry!" Ferguson yells as he runs to catch up with her. Maggie laughs at him. He is always hungry.

By now, the noonday sun is high in the sky and Ferguson's stomach keeps growling even though they just finished eating the berries.

Though the berries were mostly dried up and chewy, they still tasted good.

"I'm still hungry. Let's head back home. By the time we get back, I'll be starving!" Ferguson says.

Maggie laughs and says, "You're always hungry! I don't think anything can fill you up."

"Well," says Ferguson, "it will be nice to eat something more than berries. Then we can take a nap in the sun before we go exploring some more this afternoon."

"That sounds good to me," Maggie says.

At the same time, they look at each other and say, "I'll race you home!" and off they go—Maggie to the skies and Ferguson into the woods. He knows a shortcut and will definitely return home before Maggie.

The wind is perfect. Maggie glides in circles, around and around. She feels so free when she is flying. She knows she has a little extra time because she can fly much faster than Ferguson can run, and she will still beat him home.

Maggie continues floating on the breeze, daydreaming and not paying attention to where she is going. Looking down, she realizes Ferguson is nowhere in sight.

"Oh well," she tells herself, "I know my way back and I will still beat Ferguson home," as she laughs out loud.

CHAPTER 6

Maggie decides to fly lower and closer to the trees. As she flies around a large group of lodgepole pine trees on the other side of the lake, she looks down and sees something shiny and glittering in the water. Oh, how Maggie loves shiny things! She can't resist them. She *has* to see what it is. She knows it is something special, and she has to add it to her collection of treasures. So down she heads, straight for the water's edge.

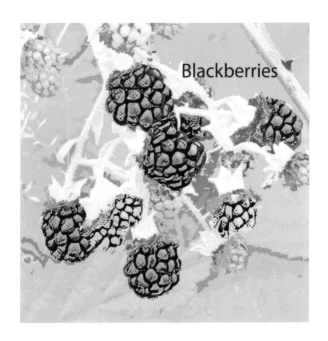

Blackberries

She is almost there when she sees several park visitors sitting on a large rock. She turns, immediately flying back to the trees. Looking around, she notices that the visitors do not see her.

They'll probably leave soon. I'll sit here and watch them, Maggie thinks to herself as she looks around to see if they are the only ones there.

After some time passes, the visitors do not leave. Maggie doesn't know how long she sits in the trees, and she wants to—she *has* to—get down to the shiny treasure. She jumps from branch to branch, getting closer and closer, and as she jumps, she becomes more excited—and impatient.

The visitors' voices and laughter echo across the water. "I wonder what they are laughing about. I know I can get closer to hear what they are saying."

She quietly continues to inch her way toward the visitors. Then she sees one of them throw something shiny into the water.

"Oh, oh, oh!" she says out loud. "Another shiny treasure. I've got to see what it is!"

Maggie hops back and forth until she can't wait any longer. She flies over to the water and snatches the first shiny treasure and quickly flies back to safety of the trees. She looks down at the visitors to see if they noticed her.

"Ah, they didn't see me," she says as she holds her treasure with her claws and begins pulling it apart with her beak.

"What is this?" she says out loud. "It's not a treasure. It's trash!" she exclaims. "Why would they throw trash into our beautiful lake? Did they do this? Is the other shiny piece trash too?"

Maggie flies to the ground and tucks the trash next to the tree trunk. She looks out to see if the visitors are watching her. They continue talking and laughing, so she carefully hops to the edge of the water. Just as she is about to grab the other shiny piece, a stone splashes in the water next to her. It startles her and she jumps!

"Maybe they didn't see me. They are probably just throwing rocks in the water," Maggie says quietly.

Lots of visitors like to skip rocks across the water. She stands at the edge of the water for another moment. It is a moment too long. Another stone is thrown, and this time, it hits her wing. It hurts so bad. She caws and caws loudly in pain and the visitors laugh.

She cannot flap her wing to fly away, so she hops back into the woods as quickly as she can to hide under the low-lying branches of the spruce trees. They throw another stone toward the trees, but the thick green branches protect her.

"Oh no, what am I going to do? How am I going to fly home? My wing hurts so much. Why do they want to hurt me? I didn't do anything to them! Why are they so mean?" All Maggie can think of while standing there shaking is, *I want to go home.*

As she looks around, she realizes she is lost and has no idea which direction to go. "Now, what do I do?" she says to herself. She knows it will take longer to get home since she doesn't know the way home from the ground.

Maggie sits quietly under the branches. The pain in her wing begins to subside. She inches her way further under the tree branches and heads deeper into the woods and away from Yellowstone Lake.

After hopping for a while, she raises her wing. "Ouch!" she cries. It hurt at first, but as she gently flaps her wing up and down, the pain slowly begins to ease. She hops up on a low-hanging branch and continues to jump from branch to branch, higher and higher in the tree.

"I've got to see if I can fly. I have to fly!" says Maggie.

With all of her determination, she leaps up and flaps her wings. She is a little unsteady at first but catches a breeze that lifts her high above the trees.

"Thank goodness!" she says. She is back where she feels safe. "Now, to find my way home."

CHAPTER 7

It has been some time since she has become separated from Ferguson. She is sure he has made it home by now and knows he will be worried, if not mad too. The most important thing at this moment is to find her way home.

As Maggie flies, she remembers how the sun looks as it lowers in the afternoon sky and how it shines on the big old fir tree that guards their den. She now knows where she is heading and soon sees familiar landscape below.

Douglas
Fir
Pinecone

She flies faster and faster as she continues looking for Ferguson, calling his name. "FERGUSON! FERGUSON!" Maggie cries. Soon she spots him. Ferguson looks up.

"Maggie, where have you been? We were together, and when I took a shortcut, I could still see you. Then you disappeared. I thought you were hurt. I've been looking all over for you!"

Ferguson yells back. He sighs with relief at the same time.

Maggie glides down and lands beside Ferguson. Keeping her composure, she says with a slight quiver in her voice, "I'm all right and I'm back home with you now."

Ferguson looks at Maggie. He looks closely and knows something is wrong. "Maggie, what happened?"

"Nothing," she says. "I was flying over a new area to explore."

But Ferguson knows better. "Maggie!"

"Okay, okay," she says.

Maggie tells him how she is having so much fun flying and floating on the breeze, and then she sees something shiny at the water's edge. She has to see what it is, and she explains in great detail that she is cautious and is staying in the safety of the trees—for a while.

"If you were so cautious, what happened to your wing?" he says.

"Oh, you noticed," Maggie replies.

Ferguson looks at her, waiting for her to continue her story. She sighs deeply and tells him about the visitors at the lake.

Ferguson sits quietly, wrapping his tail round his feet and lowering his head to look in Maggie's eyes, patiently waiting to hear everything that happen.

She continues to tell him about her shiny treasure and how she quietly makes it to the water. "The park visitors never noticed me, Ferguson." She tells him she flies back to the trees and she is so excited to look at her treasure, but it isn't a treasure at all. It's trash!

"Can you believe this?" says Maggie angrily. "They are throwing trash in our beautiful lake!" She tells him that she sees one of the visitors throw another shiny piece in the water, and she has to find out if it is trash too.

"Ferguson, I can't leave trash in our lake. It has to be picked up and thrown away."

As she continues her story, she tells him they throw a stone at her when she went back in the water the second time. They missed her the first time, but the second stone they threw hit her wing. She tells him how badly it hurt and she can't lift her wing to fly, so she hops back to the trees and hid under the thick branches.

Slowly she makes her way deeper into the woods and hops up on a low-hanging branch.

Ferguson listens until she finishes her story and looks at her a few moments before he speaks. Shaking his head, he says, "Maggie, what am I going to do with you?" He sighs and gently wraps his arms around her.

"But, Ferguson, I had to pick up that trash before it floats out into our lake!" says Maggie.

"I know, Maggie. I know you were trying to do something good, but your attraction to shiny things got you into this mess. Next time, *please*, let's go together!"

In the fading afternoon sun, they share this moment—a moment of relief, a moment of gratefulness because Maggie is safely back home, and a moment when she is so glad he is her Big Brother.

"Let's lay here and rest," Ferguson says. "A little rest, Mama's dinner, and Papa's evening story—that's what we need. Tomorrow's a new day with more adventures, and you better stay in sight!" he laughs as they settle down on a pile of warm autumn leaves in the last bit of remaining sunlight.

The sun slowly slips away and stars faintly begin to dot the edges of the evening sky. It won't be long before the moon pokes his face above the far horizon.

"Come on, Maggie, let's go home," says Ferguson.

CHAPTER 8

Chilly air fills the morning as Ferguson wakes up. It's time to get moving. With the sounds coming from the kitchen, he knows everyone is awake and breakfast will soon be ready.

Papa had to leave early this morning, so Mama says the morning prayers—thankful for Papa, her family, their home and food, and prayers for protection for Papa. While everyone is eating, Ferguson and Maggie whisper quietly, making plans for their day.

With all the chores completed, Ferguson pops out of the den with Maggie close behind. He shakes himself from his head to the tip of his fluffy tail as Maggie stretches her sore wing. Before he can ask her what she wants to do, Elvis-Anne, Lily, and Nigel (their three squirrel friends) streak by tagging him, laughing and yelling, "You're it!" and continue running as fast as they can.

Maggie laughs so hard that she topples into Ferguson, and they both fall down laughing. "The squirrels definitely want to play chase today." Maggie giggles. "I wonder where they've been. We haven't seen them lately."

Ferguson replies, "Who knows! Probably up at Grant Village begging for treats from the park visitors."

"Come on, Ferguson, you know how much I love playing chase. Those squirrels are so quick, and when they run around and around the tree trunks. They make me dizzy." Maggie giggles.

"Let's go get 'em, Little Sister." Ferguson laughs as he takes off running down the trail and Maggie to the skies.

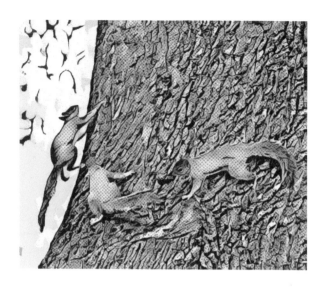

Elvis-Anne, Lily, and Nigel (who are cousins) do everything together—*everything*. They are quite the little trio. It is triple fun, and they are triple sneaky. Their favorite game is chase because they run up and down, around and around the tree trunks so fast, jump from branch to branch, and hide in holes in the trees—sometimes silently, but most of the time, they noisily laugh and chatter.

Elvis-Anne, the oldest of the squirrels, always looks out for Lily and Nigel. Oh, and yes, she is the bossy one too! She knows everyone in the woodland plus lots of great places to go exploring—and hide.

Figwort
Bush

Ferguson runs past the evergreens and rounds the next curve of the trail where it ends at a large hedge of figwort bushes. As he rounds the curve, something moves in the figwort bushes. The bush shakes back and forth. Ferguson immediately stops in his tracks, lowers his body to the ground, and quietly crawls toward the bushes. The movement stops.

"Aha," Ferguson whispers, "found you!"

He pauses for a moment, thinking about all the places he remembers the squirrels have hid, but the figwort bushes aren't one of those places. Maybe this is their new hiding place. But wait, what if it isn't the squirrels? He becomes very alert now, crouching closely to the ground with his ears straight back and his tail twitching and his heart racing!

All of a sudden, the bushes shake back and forth again. Ferguson takes a couple of steps back, and out comes a badger.

"Duff!" Ferguson says. "What a surprise!"

Duff smiles as he greets his young friend with a big warm hug. "Ferguson, my dear boy, how are you? It is so good to see you, my friend. My goodness, look how much you have grown! It's been too long since we have seen each other."

Ferguson returns the hug with his old friend. "I am doing just fine, Duff! It has been too long. What are you up to? Are you doing well?"

Duff replies, "I'm not feeling well today. I have eaten something that has made me sick and was about to go home."

After asking Duff a few questions, Ferguson says, "I will fix a concoction Mama fixes when we aren't feeling well. You'll be better in no time."

They continue their conversation. Maggie glides in and lands next to them.

Duff greets her, "Hello, Miss Maggie!" as he calls her with a smile.

Maggie smiles as she says, "Duff, you are such a gentleman!"

"Well," Duff says, "manners are important and you should be polite to a lady."

Duff is very special to Maggie. He is the Grandpa she imagined but never had.

"Thank you, Duff. How kind and thoughtful you are," says Maggie.

He walks over and gently picks her up and gives her a soft hug as she lays her head on his shoulder.

While Duff and Maggie talk, Ferguson pulls several mouthfuls of leaves from the figwort bush. Taking them over to the rocks at the edge of the stream, he lays them down and begins scratching the leaves until they are shredded into small pieces.

Maggie hops over to help Ferguson pile small rocks in a circle, making a ring in the water. After they create a little pool, they put the shredded leaves in the water. Maggie knows just what to do. She hops in and walks around and around in circles, stirring them together.

The fragrance of the shredded leaves fills the air.

Ferguson tastes the water. "It's perfect," he says as he turns to Duff. "Drink up, my friend!"

Within a short time, Duff is feeling better. The medicine has worked its magic.

Duff says, "Ferguson, my boy, tell your Mama thanks for teaching you how to make this medicine."

Their conversations continue, and Ferguson tells Duff that Elvis-Anne, Lily, and Nigel are up to their shenanigans again. "They ran past me so fast and scampered away before I could see what direction they went." Ferguson laughs.

Duff laughs a deep, hardy laugh and shakes his head. "They ran past me too. Those silly squirrels are always up to something. This is the first time I've seen them in a long time. I can't believe Elvis-Anne didn't stop to talk to me. That is so unlike her. She did holler, 'Hello Duff,' as she scampered by." He chuckles.

"Did you see which way they went?" asks Ferguson. "Those three are so sneaky and have the best hiding places."

"I'll pretend I didn't see where they went," whispers Duff.

"No, Ferguson," he says loudly, "they ran by me so fast, I don't know which way they went," while he nods his head toward a pile of rocks that have fallen from the edge of a nearby cliff.

Ferguson laughs quietly and winks at Duff. "Well, thanks, Duff. If you see them, don't let on that we have talked."

At that moment, there is a commotion in the rock pile and out runs Elvis-Anne, Lily, and Nigel. They all run off in three different directions like marbles scattering across a wood floor.

Ferguson, Maggie, and Duff burst out laughing as they listen to Elvis-Anne's laughter as they run away.

"Well, this should be more interesting!" says Ferguson.

"Are you up for a little fun, Duff?"

"Sounds great." Duff chuckles. "I'm feeling better and I can use some fun."

CHAPTER 9

"Which way do you want to go, Duff?" asks Ferguson.

"We know their favorite hiding places, so let's set a trap to catch them," says Duff.

They made their plan, and now it's time to find their scurrying little fuzzy friends. It's time for one of them to be tagged, and Ferguson is going to make sure of that!

Maggie flies just above the treetops, zigzagging back and forth as she heads from the woods by West Thumb Geyser Basin, where they live toward Grant Village.

She is excited to be going to Grant Village. It is one of the best places to explore and see the park visitors. If she sees the squirrels, she will caw loudly so Ferguson and Duff can hear her. Then she will hide in the branches to keep an eye on Elvis-Anne, Lily, and Nigel. She is going to outsmart her little friends!

"This is going to be so much fun," she says to herself as she flies faster and faster between the trees.

Duff gallops off toward the streams that flow from West Thumb Geyser Basin, at the lower west side of Yellowstone Lake, because he knows that Elvis-Anne, Lily, and Nigel love to play by those streams.

Ferguson heads from the woods by West Thumb Geyser Basin and then over to Grant Village with Maggie on the lookout. He likes when the park visitors buy fruits and snacks because he can always find a treat that someone has dropped.

As Ferguson gets closer to Grant Village, he becomes more alert, careful to stay out of sight and watch out for all the trucks and cars. He works his way around the rocks and between the trees, carefully looking left and right before quickly running across the street.

He stays close to the edge of the woods. Staying here gives him a clearer view to see if Elvis-Anne, Lily, and Nigel are playing where the visitors are. He knows how much they love looking for treats the visitors drop and begging for nuts!

As Ferguson searches and searches, he still has not spotted his furry little friends. He catches a glimpse of Maggie flying overhead. If she sees them, he will quickly know.

Ferguson makes his way past the parking lot, hurries back across the road, and cautiously makes his way to the side of a large building.

So far, so good, he thinks to himself. *Just you wait. I will find you, Elvis-Anne!*

Ferguson walks slowly around the back corner of the building, and that's when he sees them. Elvis-Anne, Lily, and Nigel all scampering around the trees that line the walking path. They are so busy looking for treats from the park visitors that they don't see Ferguson as he inches his way toward them.

He creeps slowly, going from rock to rock and then over to the trees. Elvis-Anne, Lily, and Nigel are enjoying their tasty little treats. They never notice Ferguson as he rushes up behind them and tags Elvis-Anne.

He calls out, "Got you, Elvis-Anne. You're it!" and off he runs laughing.

CHAPTER 10

Ferguson is so engrossed with his mission to find Elvis-Anne, Lily, and Nigel that he did not hear Maggie flying overhead cawing and laughing.

"You did it, Ferguson. *Great* job!"

Ferguson looks up and laughs as they both head back toward the woods.

Maggie flies ahead to find Duff by the streams. Maggie excitedly tells Duff all the details of how Ferguson tags Elvis-Anne. He laughs heartily. He isn't sure what is funnier: Maggie's version of the story or how animated she is while telling it.

Maggie continues to elaborate with exaggerating and colorful details as Ferguson walks up.

Duff is still laughing and says, "Ferguson, my boy, well done! I know those squirrels never saw you coming hahahahaha! I bet they couldn't decide for a moment whether to chase after you or finish eating the trail mix."

Ferguson laughs. "Oh, knowing those three, it's all about the treats. They'll catch up with me later."

As their laughter drifts away, Duff, Maggie, and Ferguson find a cool shady spot to sit for a little while.

The sun has shifted in the sky, and they know it's time to head home.

Maggie hugs Duff, says her goodbyes, then soars up into the breeze.

Ferguson and Duff slowly walk down the trail that runs beside the winding stream. The trail and the stream are wonderful companions, just like Ferguson and Duff.

The warm autumn muskiness hangs in the air. The sun continues to lower in the sky as clouds race on with an ever-changing adornment of colors.

Ferguson and Duff make their way across the grassland back to the hedge of the figwort bushes. They give each other a hearty hug and make plans to see each other again very soon.

As Ferguson heads toward home, Duff calls back to him, "Thank you, my boy. It was a wonderful adventure today, and it has been too long since I have had this much fun."

Ferguson smiles and shouts back, "Let's do this again soon, Duff!"

CHAPTER 11

The coolness of the evening wraps around Ferguson and Maggie. They make it home as the sun sets and closes her eyes for the day. Delicious aromas of Mama's cooking fill the air and greets them as they come inside.

"Well," says Papa, "where have you two been all day?"

As passionately as Maggie told the story to Duff about Elvis-Anne, Lily, and Nigel and their game of Chase, she begins her story again.

Ferguson jumps up and says, "Wait, Maggie! Papa, may we tell our story tonight during story time?"

Papa smiles broadly and says, "That's a wonderful idea, son. After dinner, I will build a fire, and you and Maggie can share the story of your great adventure today."

With eager excitement, they set the table. Papa brings in the firewood, and Mama calls out, "Dinner's ready!" They sit down at the table, hold each other's paws, as Papa prays a prayer of thanks to God for their family and friends, their food, and their warm home in Yellowstone National Park.

Conversation was lively while eating their dinner. Afterward, Papa builds a fire in the fireplace and they clean up the kitchen. Making their way to the big room, they sit on the floor around Papa's feet and Mama brings in her special treat of roasted nuts and dried Juneberries.

Papa clears his throat and says, "Tonight, we will start a new tradition. Ferguson, now that you are older, you can begin sharing in our family story time."

CHAPTER 12

Ferguson and Maggie are so excited! Ferguson did not know that Papa is starting a new tradition. Papa motions for both of them to come sit beside him next to the fireplace.

As the flames flicker into a steady blaze, Ferguson takes in a long slow breath and begins the telling of his and Maggie's adventures—from the moment they woke up this morning. The excitement of their story unfolds as Maggie is as animated as ever! The laughter filling their home drifts out into the night, like a song.

Ferguson is so happy as he thinks of his wonderful family, his amazing friends, and their home in the most beautiful place—Yellowstone National Park.

Papa smiles brightly and nods his head as Mama says, "We are so proud of you both. What a wonderful adventure. You are sure to have good dreams tonight."

With that, Mama ushers them off to bed as the fire burns down to glowing embers and says, "Sweet dreams, my children."

They crawl into their beds and settle in for the night.

"Thank you for a wonderful adventure today, Ferguson," Maggie says softly.

Ferguson replies, "It was great, wasn't it, Maggie? And the best part is sharing it with you, our friends, and our family."

Ferguson sighs sleepily. Looking out through his window, he sees the dark canopy of the night sky filled with twinkling stars and feathery clouds drifting across the night.

"Thank You, God, for a beautiful day and all the fun we had. Thank You most for my family and friends. Good night, God. Sweet dreams," he softly says as he drifts off to sleep.

Good night, Ferguson. Rest well and sweet dreams to you too, for there are more adventures awaiting...

ABOUT THE AUTHOR

Creativity has been Glenda Lord-Wright's journey that has led her down the path of being a graphic designer, an award-winning artist, and an award-winning photographer. That creativity has now placed her on the path of being a children's book author. So exciting!

She lives with her husband and two lovable, energetic mini-Australian shepherds, which create chaos and adventures all their own. It's a wonderful life!

CPSIA information can be obtained
at www.ICGtesting.com
Printed in the USA
LVHW071901081221
705637LV00024B/1410